Dear Parent:

Congratulations! Your child is taking the first steps on an exciting journey. The destination? Independent reading!

STEP INTO READING® will help your child get there. The program offers five steps to reading success. Each step includes fun stories and colorful art. There are also Step into Reading Sticker Books, Step into Reading Math Readers, Step into Reading Phonics Readers, Step into Reading Write-In Readers, and Step into Reading Phonics Boxed Sets—a complete literacy program with something to interest every child.

Learning to Read, Step by Step!

Ready to Read Preschool–Kindergarten
• big type and easy words • rhyme and rhythm • picture clues
For children who know the alphabet and are eager to begin reading.

Reading with Help Preschool–Grade 1
• basic vocabulary • short sentences • simple stories
For children who recognize familiar words and sound out new words with help.

Reading on Your Own Grades 1–3
• engaging characters • easy-to-follow plots • popular topics
For children who are ready to read on their own.

Reading Paragraphs Grades 2–3
• challenging vocabulary • short paragraphs • exciting stories
For newly independent readers who read simple sentences with confidence.

Ready for Chapters Grades 2–4
• chapters • longer paragraphs • full-color art
For children who want to take the plunge into chapter books but still like colorful pictures.

STEP INTO READING® is designed to give every child a successful reading experience. The grade levels are only guides. Children can progress through the steps at their own speed, developing confidence in their reading, no matter what their grade.

Remember, a lifetime love of reading starts with a single step!

For Hank and Nancy, who always eagerly await that first wintry breeze.
—*T.R.*

Visit us on the Web!
StepIntoReading.com
www.randomhouse.com/kids
Educators and librarians, for a variety of teaching tools, visit us at
www.randomhouse.com/teachers

ISBN: 978-0-7364-2836-1 (trade) — ISBN: 978-0-7364-8096-3 (lib. bdg.)

Printed in the United States of America   10 9 8 7 6 5 4 3 2

A Fairy Frost

By Tennant Redbank

Illustrated by Denise Shimabukuro
and the Disney Storybook Artists

Random House 🏠 New York

A cool breeze blew through Rani's open window. She pulled her blanket higher and snuggled down in her bed. It had gotten cold overnight. She soon began to doze off again.

All of a sudden, her eyes snapped
open. She sat straight up. Cold? Pixie
Hollow rarely got cold. The last time
was . . .

She couldn't even remember!

Just how cold was it? Rani knew one way to check.

Rani was a water-talent fairy. That meant she could make magic with water. She reached toward the water jug by her bed. She pulled a stream of water into the cold breeze. She held it there and thought ice-cold thoughts. She thought of snowflakes and slush puddles and icicles.

In a flash, the water froze in an arc over her bed.

Yes!

It was cold enough for a frost party!

Rani leaped out of bed. She dashed to her wardrobe. She found a cocoon coat and a dandelion-fluff scarf. She put them on.

Then she rushed out the door.

Rani ran all the way to the weather station. Most fairies would have flown. But Rani wasn't like most fairies. She didn't have wings. So her feet were the best way to get from place to place.

At the weather station, the weather-talent fairies were hard at work. Rani ran over to Nimbus.

"Rani, can you believe this cold snap?" he asked. He was so excited.

"It's wonderful!" Rani gushed. She grabbed his arm. "How long will it last?"

Nimbus shrugged.

"I don't know," he said. "All day? A few hours?" He looked at the sky. Clouds rushed by. "It's hard to tell."

"All day?" Rani cut in. "That's perfect!" She didn't stay any longer. She had a frost party to throw!

Rani couldn't wait to tell the other fairies and sparrow men. She came across two messenger-talent fairies, Rolo and Spring, emptying the fairy letter box.

"Today is a frost party day!" she said to them. "Let's all meet at Minnow Lake. And tell everyone to dress warmly!"

"A frost party!" Spring clapped her hands together. Letters scattered right and left. "This is the best news I've heard in ages!"

Rani went to find her fellow water-
talent fairies. She would need their help.
First she asked Silvermist.

Then Tally.

Then Spritzi and Humidia.

One after another, the water talents agreed to help. Before long, a whole row of them stood at the edge of Minnow Lake.

Around them, other fairies and sparrow men were starting to gather. They wore warm clothing—gloves, scarves, hats, and coats.

All the water talents grabbed hands. The lake looked very big. Could they really freeze it? Rani hoped this would work.

Rani closed her eyes. She squeezed Silvermist's and Tally's hands. Together, all the water-talents thought ice-cold thoughts.

Rani opened one eye a little. Nothing was happening! She closed it again and tried harder.

"Look! Look!" Rani heard Tinker Bell cry out. "It's freezing!"

Rani opened her eyes. Ice was
spreading across the top of the water!
Silvermist flew to the middle of the lake.
She landed lightly on the ice. Then she
jumped up and came down on the ice hard.
It was solid!

"Let the frost party begin!" Rani cried.

"Hooray!" Tinker Bell yelled. She was the first one to reach the lake. She slid across the ice in her slippers.

"Tink, you forgot your skates!" Prilla called.

Rosetta showed off her new hooded
pussy-willow cape. Hem had made it
for her.

"I've been waiting for just the right
day to wear it," Rosetta told Iridessa.

Fairies strapped on their ice skates. They stepped onto the lake.

Some fairies linked hands to make a long line. They played snap the whipsnake. First they skated slowly. Then they sped up.

When they made a turn, the end of the line swung out wildly. The last three fairies went tumbling heels over wings.

There was so much to do on a
frost party day! Lily and Aster made
frost flowers.

Dulcie set up a hot chocolate stand.
She handed steamy cups to the fairies who
were done skating.

Iridessa buried her face in the wide
cup. "Yum," she said.

Meanwhile, Beck asked a chipmunk friend to pull a sled. They gave rides across the ice.

Rani watched from a toadstool.
She was thrilled with the party.
Everyone was having so much fun!

She felt a tug on her arm. It was
Nimbus.

"Rani, you should know—" he started
to say. But Rani cut him off.

"Nimbus, I am so glad you came!
Did you go skating yet?" she asked.
"It's wonderful! Here. Try Dulcie's hot
chocolate!" She put a cup into his hands.

Nimbus tried again to get Rani's attention. "The wind has shifted to the south," he warned her. "Warm air is coming. Everyone should get off the ice."

Rani waved him away. Yes, it was warmer than before. But she thought the ice would hold for a while longer.

Rani said, "Just a few minutes more.
We're having so much fun!"

She hurried off for some shaved ice.
Mixie had flavored it with cherry juice.

"Rani." Nimbus caught up to her.
"I really think—"

"Duck!" Rani yelled.

Nimbus didn't duck in time. A handful
of slush splattered against his head.
It trickled down his neck.

"Tally threw it!" Rani said with a laugh. "Let's get her back." She raced off. Nimbus trailed after her.

"But Rani!" he called. "The ice!"

Rani dashed from spot to spot with Nimbus behind her. She just didn't want to listen.

But finally she gave in. Even she could feel that it was a lot warmer.

"Okay, Nimbus," she said. "I'll go ask everyone to get off the lake."

Rani skated into the middle of the ice. She stopped with a spray of crystals.

"This has been a great frost party!" she called. "But now it's over. The lake is—"

CRRRRICCCCCK.

Rani went pale. What was that sound?
She turned to look.

Oh, no!

A big crack was forming in the ice!
She had to get the fairies and sparrow men
off the melting lake. Because they have
wings, fairies can't swim!

Rani skated quickly toward a cluster of fairies. "Fly away!" she shouted. "Fly away!"

The crack zigzagged across the ice.

Rani skated to another group, and another and another. "Fly away!" she yelled over and over again.

Like a flock of swallows, all the fairies lifted off the ice. They made it just in time. Seconds later, the ice broke apart.

Of course, there was one fairy who couldn't fly, because she didn't have wings: Rani.

She dropped through the broken ice like a stone.

Everyone gasped, then held their breath. What would happen?

Before anyone could move, Rani's head poked out of the lake. She blew a stream of water between her lips.

The fairies let out their pent-up breath. They had forgotten. Rani couldn't fly . . . but she could swim!

Rani swam to the edge of the lake and got out. Nimbus wrapped a blanket around her shoulders and handed her a cup of hot chocolate.

"You were right, Rani," he said. "It was a great day for a frost party."

"Yes, it was!" Rani said. Then she grinned and pulled the blanket tighter. "But it was an awfully cold day for a swim!"